PRIDE OF THE GREEN MOUNTAINS

This book is part of the

TREASURED HORSES COLLECTION™

that is distributed with replica horses

in toy and hobby stores by

The ERTL Company, Incorporated.

Read all of the books in the

TREASURED HORSES COLLECTION™

Pride of the Green Mountains (Morgan)

Ride of Courage (Arabian)

Kate's Secret Plan (Quarter Horse)

Riding School Rivals (Lipizzan)

Spirit of the West (Appaloosa)

Changing Times (Tennessee Walking Horse)

Colorado Summer (Paint Horse)

Pretty Lady of Saratoga (Thoroughbred)

Christmas in Silver Lake (Clydesdale)

The Stallion of Box Canyon (Mustang)

PRIDE OF THE GREEN MOUNTAINS

The story of a trusty Morgan horse and the girl who turns to him for help

Written by Carin Greenberg Baker
Illustrated by Sandy Rabinowitz
Cover Illustration by Christa Keiffer
Developed by Nancy Hall, Inc.

SCHOLASTIC INC.
New York Toronto London Auckland Sydney

ISBN 0-590-31654-0

 Published by Scholastic Inc., 555 Broadway, New York, NY 10012, by arrangement with Nancy Hall, Inc. and The ERTL Company.

12 11 10 9 8 7 6 5 3/0

Printed in the U.S.A. 40
First Scholastic printing, October 1997

The author gratefully acknowledges the staff of the National Museum of the Morgan Horse, in Shelburne, Vermont, for their help with this book.

CONTENTS

CHAPTER 1 *The Spelling Lesson* 9

CHAPTER 2 *Mother's News* 22

CHAPTER 3 *A Good Friend* 34

CHAPTER 4 *Mr. Green* 44

CHAPTER 5 *Rosalie's Idea* 53

CHAPTER 6 *Rosalie Strikes a Deal* 63

CHAPTER 7 *A Hard Day's Work* 76

CHAPTER 8 *The Race* 85

CHAPTER 9 *Doing What's Right* 92

CHAPTER 10 *At Long Last* 97

EPILOGUE 111

FACTS ABOUT THE BREED 119

The Spelling Lesson

"Persevere. P-e-r, per," recited seven-year-old Mathilda Goodman from the front of the one-room classroom. "S-e-v, sev," she continued in her high, sweet voice, rocking back and forth in her little black leather boots. "E-r-e, ere," she finished proudly. The teacher, Miss Nelson, nodded and smiled. Mathilda was a good speller. She was good in reading and arithmetic and history, too.

Not like me, thought Mathilda's older sister, Rosalie, who sat further back in the classroom. Though Rosalie was ten, she could barely keep up in any of her lessons. It wasn't that she was stupid, her mother was always saying. The problem was that she spent too much of her time daydreaming about horses, and about one horse in particular.

Miss Nelson glanced into her blue-back speller and then pointed her wooden ruler at Cassie Howard. Ten-year-old Cassie, Rosalie's best friend, sat beside her on the long wooden bench. Tall and thin, she had blue-green eyes and straight blond hair pulled back in a long, neat braid. "Spell *tolerance*," the teacher directed Cassie.

Cassie stood up, towering over Rosalie. "Tolerance. T-a-l-l . . ."

Miss Nelson laughed. "Tall? You must be describing yourself!"

Several children in the class snickered, and Cassie's face grew very red. Rosalie reached for Cassie's hand and gave it a squeeze. Cassie was self-conscious about being so tall, and it didn't help that people made fun of her. Especially the teacher!

Rosalie frowned at the young woman who sat behind her desk on the raised platform in front of the class. Rosalie wasn't fooled by the teacher's upswept hair or her long fitted dress with its fancy braided trim. A few years ago, "Miss" Nelson was just Connie Nelson, one of the bigger girls at the back of the classroom. A teaching certificate didn't make her grown-up, and it didn't give her the right to be mean.

No wonder a lot of the kids called her "Nasty Nelson."

"Rosalie Goodman," Miss Nelson called, as she rose and walked down the aisle toward Rosalie.

Rosalie slowly stood up and looked at her teacher.

"Spell *cavalry*," Miss Nelson said.

Rosalie smiled. Bad as she was in school, this was a word she could spell backward and forward. Rosalie's father, Aaron Goodman, was a soldier in the First Vermont Cavalry, a regiment on horseback that had ridden off to fight the Civil War. He had left in December of 1861, nearly three years ago, riding off on his chestnut Morgan horse, Captain. He'd looked so handsome and proud in his blue uniform with shiny brass buttons. Captain looked just as ready to fight, with his gleaming, muscular body, huge, alert eyes, and tiny, eager ears.

Rosalie had tried to keep this picture in her mind. She'd tried to remind herself that her father and Captain were fighting the battle against slavery and were trying to make the country whole again. But the picture had faded, especially in the last few months when she hadn't received even one letter from her father. Before now, Aaron Goodman had never gone more than two weeks without writing.

Rosalie's mother kept saying that the mails were unpredictable in wartime, but Rosalie could see the worry in her mother's eyes. Rosalie knew her mother was thinking the same thing she was thinking. What if something had happened to Father? What if he was sick or injured or even worse?

Miss Nelson spoke again, bringing Rosalie's thoughts back to the drafty room with its long wooden benches and cast-iron stove belching smoke. "Were you planning to answer *today*," the teacher asked Rosalie, "or do you need a rap on the knuckles to wake you up?"

Some of Rosalie's classmates laughed.

Rosalie gritted her teeth. Connie Nelson wasn't going to make fun of her and get away with it. "Cavalry," Rosalie said in a loud, clear voice. "C-a-v, cav, a-l, al, r-y, ry." Miss Nelson barely nodded as she turned to the next pupil. "Erastus Woodward, spell *sacrifice*."

"My! I'm glad *that's* over with," Cassie said to Rosalie as the two of them hurried down the school's back stairs into the autumn sunshine.

The school sat at the top of a hill surrounded by maple trees, their branches nearly bare except for a few dry brown leaves. Through the branches, Rosalie could see the gentle curve of the Green Mountains in the distance, dark against the light gray sky.

"Do you want to come over to my house and play

with Suzette and Mimi?" Cassie asked. Suzette and Mimi were the new dolls Cassie had received for her birthday. They were beautiful, made of porcelain with handpainted faces, lacy dresses and real leather shoes. One of them, Suzette, even looked exactly like Rosalie with its pale white skin, chocolate-brown eyes, and dark curly hair. But Rosalie didn't have time to play after school.

"I'm sorry," Rosalie told her friend, "but I've got to take Mathilda and Albert straight home and start the milking."

Albert, Rosalie's nine-year-old brother, was still in the cloakroom with Mathilda. Rosalie and her brother and sister lived on a dairy farm just a few miles outside the town of Morrisville, Vermont. They'd always helped out with the chores, and now that their father was away fighting the war they had even more work to do. Even so, that wasn't the main reason Rosalie was in such a hurry to get home. Her *other* best friend was waiting for her there.

"I'll see you tomorrow," Rosalie promised Cassie.

Mathilda and Albert were coming down the stairs, bundled up against the chilly wind. Rosalie grabbed their hands and almost pulled them down the dirt road that led out of town. A few miles down the road, she turned in at the wooden gate. Leaving her brother and sister behind, she ran past the neat, two-story white farmhouse with its green wooden shutters. She barely glanced at the field where the cows were grazing on what was left of the grass. She headed straight for the barn. Throwing open the door, she ran over the hard-packed earth past the cows' empty stalls. Dodging chickens and the barn cat, Whisper, she finally reached her favorite place in all the world.

"Major!" Rosalie cried joyfully, greeting the Morgan horse who looked over the door of his stall. Major was a bay, brown with a black mane and tail. He was a small, heavily muscled horse with a clean-cut head, proudly crested neck, and powerful shoulders. He whinnied and touched Rosalie's cheek with his soft, velvety nose. Rosalie nestled against the horse's muzzle. Being with Major made her forget all about school and Miss Nelson's meanness and almost made her forget how much she missed her father.

Major, Captain's older brother, was ten years old, just like Rosalie. Their birthdays were less than one week apart. Even before she could walk, Rosalie had sat astride Major's broad, strong back while her father led them by a rope. Major had always been gentle with her, and when she grew older and more experienced as a rider, he'd taken her for wild gallops along the banks of the Lamoille River.

But Major wasn't just a riding horse. Major probably worked harder on the farm than Rosalie, or her mother and father, or Ed, the field hand. Major pulled the plow during spring planting and pulled the mower in the summer when they harvested the hay. When Rosalie's father drove to Burlington to pick up supplies, Major pulled the heavy wagon. Hard as he worked, though, Major was never too tired to listen when Rosalie had a problem. Rosalie knew he couldn't really understand her words, but she was sure he sensed how she felt.

Major pushed his nose into the pocket of Rosalie's jacket. Rosalie laughed. She'd saved her sugar cookie from lunch as a treat for the horse. Rosalie had wanted it to be a surprise, but there was no fooling Major. Major's lips tickled Rosalie's palm as he delicately picked up the cookie from her hand.

"Ready to go to work?" Rosalie asked as she opened the door to Major's stall.

Major stamped his hooves and threw back his head.

Rosalie took a lead rope off a wooden peg and hitched it to one side of Major's halter. Then she grabbed a woolen saddle blanket that hung over a metal rail and threw it over Major's back. After leading Major out of the barn, Rosalie stepped up on a wooden block beside him. Pulling herself up onto Major's back, she rode him out into the pasture. Rosalie often rode Major bareback. She felt much closer to him that way.

Rosalie touched her heels against Major's sides, and he broke into a canter toward the open field where the cows were grazing.

"Hiyup!" Rosalie shouted as she and Major curved to the right around the herd.

Most of the cows started moving toward the barn, but two young cows, Homer and Clarence, galloped away toward the road that ran beside the field. Rosalie sighed. Those two never wanted to come inside. They wanted to stay outside and play all day.

"Let's get 'em, Major!" Rosalie shouted.

Major took off after the cows at a brisk trot. Hearing the sound of hooves behind him, Homer looked back over his shoulder. Then he cut quickly to the left while Clarence veered off to the right.

"Pretty clever," Rosalie said to Major.

The cows were smart, but Major was smarter, and he could run a lot faster than either one of them. Picking up the pace, Major raced past Clarence and turned to face him, lowering his head so he was staring right into Clarence's mischievous brown eyes. Clarence planted his hooves and stared right back.

Then, suddenly, Clarence darted to the right. Major moved even more quickly, putting himself in Clarence's way again. Clarence bolted to the left, but Major was waiting for him. Major pushed his nose closer to Clarence's, daring him to try any more tricks. With a frustrated snort, Clarence turned around and jogged toward the barn. Homer, who always did what Clarence did, followed close behind.

"That's some big spirit for a little horse," said an admiring voice.

Rosalie turned and saw a heavyset man standing by the fence that separated the field from the road. He had a thick brown beard and mustache and wore a dark suit and hat. Rosalie had never seen him before.

"Is he as strong as he looks?" the man asked.

Rosalie nodded proudly. "My daddy says that Major could pull the Vermont Central Railroad all by himself."

The man nodded and smiled. "I'm new here," he said. "The name's Joseph Green. I just bought the farm down the road. That is, if you can call it a farm. Looks more like a forest right now. I don't know how I'm going to clear the land by spring."

Clarence, who'd almost made it to the barn, suddenly decided to make one last break for freedom. He went running toward the woods on the other side

of the field.

"I'm sorry, but I have to go!" Rosalie said, galloping after Clarence. "Pleased to meet you, Mr. Green."

After all the cows were in their stalls, Rosalie turned Major loose for a roll in the pasture. Then she joined Albert and Mathilda, who'd already started the milking. Rosalie sat down on a stool beside Tillie, Clarence's mother.

Splish! Splash! Splish! Splash!

The creamy white liquid hitting the pail made a comforting sound as Rosalie started milking Tillie. Angry voices outside the barn, however, broke the peaceful moment. Rosalie couldn't make out the words, but she could tell that her mother was talking to Ed, their field hand.

Peering between two boards in the barn wall, Rosalie could see her mother with Ed, a lean, wiry man with leathery brown skin.

Ed looked angry and Rosalie's mother looked worried. Ed kept waving his arms, and Rosalie's mother kept shaking her head. Then Ed stormed away, and Rosalie's mother mopped at her eyes with the corner of her apron.

Rosalie's heart was gripped with a cold fear. Why

was her mother crying? Had something happened to her father? Rosalie was tempted to run to the barn door and call to her mother, asking what was wrong, but she didn't want to worry her younger brother and sister. Rosalie decided to speak to her mother alone the first chance she got.

Mother's News

"And when we got to the four-syllable words, I was the only one who spelled my word correctly," Mathilda bragged a few hours later as she dried the supper dishes. "Industrious. I-n, in. D-u-s, dus. T-r-i, tri. O-u-s, ous."

"Except for Erastus Woodward," Rosalie pointed out. She stood a few feet away from her little sister, washing the dishes in the kitchen sink. The Goodmans' kitchen was a large, plain room with whitewashed walls and a wood floor. A large pine table filled the center of the room with a variety of chairs gathered around it. A cast-iron, woodburning cookstove stood near one wall next to a pantry closet filled with bins of flour and sugar, jars of preserves, and other stored food. The room was dimly lit by an oil lamp which sat on a lace doily in the center of the table.

"Erastus spelled *disrespectful*," Mathilda said, turning up her nose. "That's just *disrespect* with *ful* on the end."

"Erastus Woodward is a little weasel," Albert said as he entered the kitchen carrying a pile of firewood. "I could knock him down with one hand tied behind my back."

"Albert!" said their mother, who sat at the table mending stockings. "That's no way to talk."

"He *is* a weasel," Albert insisted, dumping his pile of wood in a bin next to the stove. "Just like his father. A coward." Erastus's father was one of the few men in town who hadn't volunteered to serve in the Union Army.

Rosalie sighed. She knew another reason Albert was mad at Erastus and his father. Albert was mad because Erastus had a father who still lived at home with his family. Which was more than Albert or any of the Goodmans could say. Rosalie glanced over at her mother, who frowned at the black stocking in her hand. Her forehead was all bunched together and her lips were thin and tight. She'd barely said a word at supper, either, mostly pushing food around on her plate and asking if anybody wanted more to eat.

This was unlike the way she'd been before the war, before Daddy had gone away. Back then, Rosalie's mother was always talking, singing, or laughing. Now she rarely even smiled. But never, before today, had Rosalie seen her mother so little interested in food. That had to mean there was something very, very wrong.

"I'll finish up the drying," Rosalie offered Mathilda. "You go upstairs and do your schoolwork."

"You don't have to ask me twice," Mathilda said happily, tossing her dish towel at Rosalie. Mathilda, much to Rosalie's amazement, loved practicing her multiplication tables and memorizing long, boring passages from *McGuffey's Reader*. And tonight Rosalie was especially glad of it, because it got Mathilda out of the room so Rosalie could talk to her mother. Now she just had to get rid of Albert.

"Do you know your state capitals for tomorrow?" she asked her brother. "Nasty Nelson's going to test us."

Albert started singing to the tune of "Yankee Doodle Dandy." "State of Maine, Augu-us-ta, Massachusetts, Springfield . . ." Everyone sang this song to help them remember the capitals, but Albert hadn't gotten any further than the first two.

"You'd better get upstairs," Rosalie prompted her brother.

Albert made a face, but he scurried up the stairs after Mathilda.

As soon as her brother and sister were gone, Rosalie hurried to her mother's side and pulled up a chair beside her. "Mama," she said, laying a hand on her mother's knee. "What's wrong?" Rachel Goodman smiled with her mouth, but her eyes were wide and scared. "Nothing, Rosie," she said. "There's nothing for you to worry about."

Rosalie knew her mother was trying to protect her from something. "Please, Mama," she insisted. "You can tell me. I'm not a little girl anymore."

Rosalie's mother looked as if she were about to cry. "I know this war has been hard on you," she said, "and you've grown up a lot since your daddy went away. You've been so good about helping me with everything and looking after your younger brother and sister. But you *are* still a little girl, and I'd like to keep it that way."

Rosalie felt a lump rise in her throat. The news must be even worse than she'd thought. "Is Daddy. . ." The thought was so horrible she couldn't even say the word.

Rachel Goodman looked shocked. "Oh, no!" she said, leaning forward and throwing her arms around Rosalie. "It's got nothing to do with your daddy. It's about the farm."

Rosalie rested her head against her mother's shoulder. She almost felt safe, surrounded by her mother's loving arms. But even though she was relieved the worst hadn't happened, the problem still had to be pretty serious. "What's the matter with the farm?" Rosalie asked. "Maybe there's something I can help you with."

"I guess I'm going to have to tell you one way or the other." Rachel took a deep breath then fixed her dark eyes on Rosalie's. "We've been having money problems," she said. "Terrible problems. Do you remember last spring, when so many of our cows got sick and died?"

"Pleuropneumonia," Rosalie recalled. That had been an awful time. They'd lost nearly half the herd, which meant there'd been a lot less milk, and a lot less cheese and butter. And selling cheese and butter was how the Goodmans made most of their money.

"Our taxes have gone up, too, because of the war," Rachel Goodman went on, "but the big problem is the mortgage."

Rosalie had heard the word *mortgage* before when

her parents were talking together late at night, but she'd never really understood what it meant. She thought it had something to do with a bank and something to do with their farm, but that was about all she knew.

"A mortgage is a loan," her mother explained. "The bank lent us money so we could buy the farm. Now we have to pay them back twenty dollars every month. We were all right before the war, paying back everything on time, but it's so much harder now with your daddy gone and losing all those cows."

Rosalie was starting to get an idea of what the problem was. "You mean we don't have enough money to pay the bank?"

Rosalie's mother nodded. "The mortgage payment's due in thirty days and I don't have any idea where the money's going to come from. I also haven't been able to pay Ed for a couple of months, and he's not going to stay much longer."

Rosalie's body was starting to feel heavier, weighing her down in the wooden chair. "What are we going to do?" she asked her mother.

Rachel got up from her chair and walked over to the cookstove, where she threw another log on the dying flames. She stood for a moment facing the stove with her hands outstretched to warm them. Then she turned to face Rosalie. "I have a solution," she said quietly, "but you're not going to like it."

Rosalie wanted to get up and run away, but her legs and arms felt like lead.

"We're going to have to let Ed go," Rachel Goodman continued. "The hay's been harvested and winter's coming, so we won't need anyone, really, until the spring planting."

"But what about all the other things he does?" Rosalie asked. "Who's going to chop the wood and clean the stables and build the fences and everything else?"

Rachel hung her head, and in that small gesture Rosalie knew the answer to her question.

"Us?" Rosalie asked, not wanting to believe it. "Albert and Mathilda and me?"

Rachel nodded.

"But doing all those things will take all day!" Rosalie protested. "We'd have to drop out of school!"

"I know," Rosalie's mother said. "And believe me, I hate to do this. I want all of you to get a good education. But I have no choice! And I promise, as soon as we're on our feet again, you'll go right back."

Rosalie felt hot tears fill her eyes. Much as she couldn't stand Nasty Nelson, and much as she felt bored and frustrated by school, she didn't want to be uneducated all her life. Rosalie dreamed of moving to a big city such as Burlington or Montpelier someday, or maybe even Boston. Major would come with her, of course, and the two of them would live together, Rosalie in a fine house with a fancy parlor and a bathing room upstairs with hot water that came through a pipe in the wall. Major would live in a beautiful stable right next door, filled with oats and hay and a beautiful leather saddle from Moseman's catalogue for him to wear. But it looked as though none of that was going to happen now. Rosalie would probably end up stuck here in Morrisville.

Rosalie wanted to sink through the floor and burrow into the earth below. But she couldn't do that. Her mother needed help and she was the only one to give it. And she wasn't just helping her mother. Rosalie liked to think that if she did her very best to keep the farm going, it would somehow help her father get home more quickly, or keep him safe wherever he was.

Another thought was starting to nag at her. Another money problem. Something that wasn't going to go away. Then Rosalie realized what it was.

"What about the mortgage payments?" Rosalie asked her mother. "Even if we all work on the farm, we won't be making any more money. How are we going to pay the bank each month?"

Rosalie's mother came back to the table and sat beside Rosalie. "There's only one way I can think of," she said softly. "We're going to have to sell Major."

Rosalie couldn't believe her ears. She must be dreaming. She wasn't really sitting in the kitchen, staring through teary eyes at the pots and pans stacked on the wooden shelf by the stove. Her mother wasn't sitting just inches away with tears in her own eyes, squeezing her hand. Rosalie must be curled up in the hay in Major's stall, fast asleep, having a nightmare. Any minute now, Major would wake her up with the soft touch of his lips on her cheek.

"Rosalie," her mother said, holding her shoulders. "Rosalie . . ."

The fingers pressing into her shoulders brought Rosalie back to the chilly kitchen with its flickering oil light.

"You can't do it," Rosalie pleaded with her mother. "You can't sell Major! He's . . . he's part of our family. You might as well sell me, or Albert, or Mathilda!"

"I know that's how you feel," Rachel said, "but it's not really the same thing. Major's just an animal."

"That's not true!" Rosalie exclaimed. "He's my friend. And he works so hard for us. *This* is how you thank him? By *selling* him?"

Rachel's face looked sad but determined. "I'm sorry, Rosie," she said, "but we are absolutely desperate. And now that the haying is finished, we can do without a horse until the spring planting. Or we can always rent a team of oxen. And we'll have another Morgan when Daddy returns with Captain."

Rachel's voice, which had started out so firm and strong, broke at the end. Rosalie knew why. Though her mother had said "*when* Daddy returns," what she really meant was *if. If* her father ever returned.

The tears which had been swimming for so long in front of Rosalie's eyes now spilled down all over her face. She had to get out of this kitchen, away from her mother, to the only place left where she could feel any comfort at all. Rosalie ran to the door, threw it open, and flung herself into the cold night air even though she wore no jacket or coat. Running for the barn, she stumbled through the dark to Major's stall where he stood, patiently, as if waiting for her.

"Oh, Major!" Rosalie cried, throwing her arms around his neck and burying her face in his soft coat. She couldn't find words to tell him how awful things were. No word from Father, no more school, and worst of all, no more Major! But Major seemed to understand without words. His heart beat regularly beneath his solid chest, sending pulses of comfort into

Rosalie's weary body. He inclined his head toward hers and softly rubbed his cheek against hers.

She can't sell you, Rosalie thought, not daring to say the words aloud for fear Major would understand. *I won't let her.* There had to be some way to stop her mother from going through with this terrible mistake. Rosalie had no idea what she could do, but she was determined to think of something.

A Good Friend

"Come on, Major," Rosalie told her horse. "We're getting out of here."

Rosalie led the Morgan out of his stall, grabbed his saddle blanket, and threw it over his back. Then she lifted up the worn leather saddle that perched on a wooden sawhorse. The saddle had belonged to her father when he was a boy and was worn to a smooth shine. It was just the right size for Rosalie. She placed the saddle on Major's back and slid it back a few inches to make sure all the hairs underneath were lying flat. Then she did up the girth. Finally, she brought out Major's bridle. He put his head down and eagerly took the bit in his mouth while she slipped the crown piece over his ears. He seemed to sense Rosalie's urgent need to leave and, as always, he was ready for anything.

Although Rosalie knew she shouldn't leave her mother without a word, she hopped onto Major's back. Rosalie squeezed her calves against the horse's sides and they took off, out of the barn and into the starless night. They galloped down the road toward town, Major's hooves hitting the ground with a steady beat. Only the moon lit their path, shining through a veil of clouds.

Rosalie and Major slowed when they reached town, and Rosalie guided Major to the right, down Main Street. Oil lamps lit windows in some of the houses, but most of the stores were dark and shuttered. Rosalie had passed them all so many times, however, that she recognized them as easily as if it were daylight.

There was Decker's General Store with its false two-story front. Decker's was little more than one big room with a porch in front, but everyone agreed the second story made the store look more important, like something you'd see in a big city. Next to Decker's was the blacksmith's, and next to that was Morrisville Savings & Loan. Ordinarily, when Rosalie passed the bank, she didn't give it a thought. Tonight, however, the dark building with its tall white columns seemed like the head of a wolf with its jaws open, revealing long, sharp fangs, ready to devour her and her family.

Rosalie shuddered and urged Major on. The barbershop was straight ahead, and that was where Rosalie was heading. Cassie's father was the town barber, and the family lived in a house right next to his shop. Warm light filled the lace curtained windows, lamplight mixed with flickering firelight. The sound of a piano and singing could be heard, floating into the chilly night air.

Rosalie hopped off Major's back and tied him to a hitching post in front of the barbershop. "Don't worry," she told her horse, kissing his nose. "I won't be long."

Rosalie knocked on the Howards' front door. Seconds later, she heard light footsteps, and the door opened. Anna Lenox, the Howards' hired girl, held an oil lamp up to see who was at the door. Anna was thirteen, and she'd used to go to school with Rosalie. When Anna hadn't come back one September and had started working for the Howards, Rosalie hadn't given it a moment's thought. But now, staring into Anna's tired face, Rosalie suddenly saw herself.

"Rosalie! What are you doing here so late?" Anna asked, leading Rosalie into the entrance hall. "Does your mama know you're out?"

"Yes," Rosalie lied, "she sent me on an errand in town. I was just stopping by on my way home."

Anna shrugged and led Rosalie down the carpeted hall, past a mirrored hallstand and a marble-top table. The sound of piano playing and singing was getting louder. Anna paused by the doorway that led into the Howards' back parlor.

"They're all singing in the back parlor," Anna said. Without waiting for any response, she brushed past Rosalie, and went back down the hall toward the kitchen.

Rosalie peeked into the Howards' back parlor. It wasn't fancy like their front parlor, but was more of a comfortable family room. The walls were papered with lilacs and roses, and several sturdy cabinets held magazines, newspapers, and games. The comfortable-looking leather chair in one corner with a pipe stand beside it was Mr. Howard's favorite place for reading the newspaper. Mrs. Howard's rocking chair sat in a corner beside a small round table with her sewing basket. In the center of the room was a big oval table, currently covered by a half-completed jigsaw puzzle.

In another corner of the room, the entire Howard family was singing around the upright piano while Mrs. Howard played. She was a tall, angular woman whose gingham dress hung loosely over her bony frame. Mr. Howard was also tall and lanky. He was missing two fingers on his left hand, thanks to a shell fragment that had struck him when he was serving in the Tenth Vermont. Everyone in town had thought he'd never be able to go back to barbering, but he'd managed to work around his injury and still could give the best haircuts for miles around.

Cassie's fourteen-year-old sister, Sarah, wasn't as tall as the rest of the family, but she was slender and graceful. Cassie, standing beside Sarah, was already several inches taller than her older sister. She sang in a loud, clear voice, proud of the sound. While Cassie was usually shy and self-conscious, she was completely sure of herself when she sang. Occasionally, her father would glance over at her and smile.

Rosalie felt a pain in her chest as she watched the Howards, all together in their comfortable home. She remembered how her own family used to gather around the kitchen table after dinner, listening while her mother or father read a book aloud. The way things looked now, they might not even *have* a kitchen because they wouldn't have a house—unless they sold Major.

The song ended, and Cassie noticed Rosalie

standing in the doorway. "Rosalie!" she exclaimed. "What are you doing here so late?"

Mr. and Mrs. Howard and Sarah also turned and looked at her curiously.

"I was just passing by," Rosalie said brightly, trying to smile. "Would it be all right if I spoke to Cassie for a minute?"

Mrs. Howard nodded. "I'll have Anna bring some milk and cookies to Cassie's room."

Cassie bounded over the diamond-patterned carpet and grabbed Rosalie's hand. "Come on," she said, leading Rosalie back down the hall.

Cassie's room was small and narrow, with just enough room for a single bed, a dresser, a washstand, and a glass cabinet filled with Cassie's doll collection. Suzette and Mimi had the place of honor in the center of the top shelf, surrounded by a dozen others, ranging from some smaller porcelain dolls with fancy dresses to an old, battered rag doll that had belonged to Cassie when she was a baby.

"What's the matter?" Cassie asked, leading Rosalie to the bed where they sank into the soft feather mattress.

"My mother's going to sell Major!" Rosalie blurted out.

Cassie gasped. "How could she? I mean, why

would she do something like that?"

Rosalie tried to explain about the mortgage and the taxes, and even though she was sure she didn't say it right, Cassie understood immediately.

"But there's got to be some other way to get the money," Cassie insisted.

"That's why I'm here," Rosalie said. "I knew you'd help me think of something."

"Good!" said Cassie confidently. She leaned forward and reached underneath her mattress, where she fished around for a moment. "Found it!" she exclaimed, pulling out a small silk pouch. Opening it, she took out five silver dollars. "Here," she said, handing them to Rosalie. "I've saved these up from birthdays and Christmas. You can have all of it, and you don't even have to pay me back."

There had been many times that night when Rosalie had wanted to cry, and she'd only given in to tears once. But now, seeing how generous and wonderful her best friend was, Rosalie burst into tears again.

Cassie patted her back softly, and Rosalie cried until her eyes were so swollen she could hardly see. When she finally stopped and looked up, she saw that two glasses of milk and a plate of cookies had appeared on the dresser. Rosalie felt even worse when she saw them. Anna must have brought them in while she was crying, which meant now the whole Howard family knew something was wrong.

"This is so nice of you," Rosalie said to Cassie, handing back the silver dollars, "but we owe much more than this. And I can't take it from you, anyway. I've got to come up with my own solution."

Cassie put the coins back in their pouch. "All right," she said. "Let's think of something. Is there anything else you can sell? Anything of value?"

Rosalie thought hard. She had a silver-handled hairbrush that had been passed down in her family for many years. Rosalie loved it, but she would have parted with it in a minute if she had thought her mother wouldn't find out. She had a gold locket, containing a picture of her father, which she always wore around her neck. Rosalie opened the locket, now, and stared at the tiny picture. Her father stared back under bushy black eyebrows, his full lips practically buried beneath a thick mustache. She could sell the locket, and keep the picture, but that would only fetch a dollar at the most. And what would she do even if she sold everything she owned? It still wouldn't cover one month's mortgage payment. And the mortgage wasn't due just this month. It was due *every* month.

Rosalie shook her head. "I've got to find some steady income," she said. "But I wouldn't even be able to go out and work because my mother's letting Ed go. Albert and Mathilda and I are going to have to work on the farm."

Cassie shook her head, disbelieving. "Poor Rosalie! There has to be *something* we can do! Let's think hard."

Rosalie and Cassie sat and thought for a full fifteen minutes with neither of them saying a word. At last, Cassie sighed and her shoulders slumped. "I'm sorry," she said, her own eyes full of tears. "I feel like an awful friend, 'cause I can't think of anything."

"You're not an awful friend," Rosalie said fiercely. "You're the best! I'm sure I can come up with something. And now I'd better get going."

Rosalie rose quickly and hurried out of the room, past the uneaten cookies and the untouched glasses of milk. Though she could see Cassie's sister and parents peering with concern from the back parlor, she just waved to them and hurried down the stairs to the street where Major was waiting. She unhitched her horse and hopped up on his back. Major took off down the rutted street, jolting Rosalie with every step. Now that she was alone, she could admit to herself what she hadn't been able to say to her friend. There was no alternative. They'd have to sell Major, and there wasn't a thing she could do about it.

Mr. Green

Rosalie sat on Major's back, riding him slowly in a circle in the pasture. The ground seemed far away, but Major's back was big and wide. Rosalie knew she didn't have to be afraid of falling.

A long rope was tied to Major's halter. Rosalie's father was holding onto the other end of the rope, smiling encouragement at Rosalie as she rode Major around him. Daddy was wearing baggy brown denim pants held up by those bright red suspenders that Mama had bought him as a joke. Mama never thought he would wear such silly colored suspenders, but he had, nearly every day, probably just to tease her. Mama and Daddy were always teasing each other.

"He's a wonderful little horse," Daddy was saying. "I haven't seen anything like him in three counties."

Something seemed odd. Daddy hadn't worn those suspenders since Rosalie was a little girl. The suspenders had broken, and he'd thrown them away. So how could he be wearing them now? And it had been years since Daddy had trained Rosalie to ride. In any case, Daddy couldn't be here now. Daddy was off fighting the war.

Rosalie opened her eyes and realized she was lying in bed, under her patchwork quilt. The morning light was pale and uncertain, almost as if the sun hadn't yet made up its mind to rise. Mathilda, fast asleep beside her, was buried deep under the covers, with only a small shock of black hair showing.

"He certainly is a fine horse," Rosalie's mother's voice wafted up the stairs. "And it's hard to find one these days, with the war on."

"I know," a man's voice said. "I've been looking."

Rosalie sat straight up in bed. It was the same voice she'd heard in her dream. But it couldn't be Daddy downstairs, could it? Could he really have come home from the war? Maybe that was why he hadn't written. Maybe he wanted to surprise everyone! Rosalie hopped out of bed, shivering against the cold, and threw her dress on over her nightgown. Stuffing her feet into her boots, she ran downstairs.

Rosalie raced into the kitchen. "Daddy!" she

started to say, but the words froze on her lips when she saw whom her mother was talking to. It wasn't Daddy. It was Joseph Green, the man who'd bought the farm next door. "I'd like to take a closer look at him," Mr. Green was saying, "before I make my decision."

"Of course," Rachel Goodman said. "He's in the barn."

Now it was all painfully clear to Rosalie. Not only was this not her father, but the reason Mr. Green was here was to buy Major! The events of the past evening crowded Rosalie's heart and she hung her head remembering the worry she had caused her mother.

"No!" Rosalie whispered. "You can't sell him!"

Rosalie's mother gave her a harsh look, but Mr. Green looked sympathetic. "I can see how much you love that horse," he said. "But if I buy him, you're welcome to come visit."

Rosalie knew Mr. Green was trying to be nice, but he couldn't realize how cruel he sounded. Visit her horse? Her own horse?

Rosalie trailed after her mother and Mr. Green as they walked outside to the barn. Major was in his stall, chewing calmly on his hay. Rachel Goodman opened the stall door and led Major out into the passageway.

Mr. Green stroked Major's smooth neck. Then he rubbed his hands against Major's back and hindquarters and felt each of his legs and feet. Major stood there patiently, still chewing. "He looks sound," Mr. Green observed. "Has a sweet disposition, too."

For once, Rosalie wished her horse weren't so obviously superior to every other horse in the world. This was making it much too easy for Mr. Green to want to buy him.

Mr. Green opened Major's mouth and looked inside at the horse's teeth. Rosalie knew what Mr. Green was doing. He was trying to see how old Major was. You could tell by looking for a groove on one of the horse's teeth. The groove usually appeared when a horse was nine years old and then kept moving down the tooth as the horse got older.

"He's ten years old," said Mrs. Goodman, who also knew what Mr. Green was looking for. "His father lived to be thirty and did the work of a draft team almost to the very end."

"I've heard that about Morgans,"Mr. Green said. "I just wonder if he's too small for the job I have in mind."

"What job is that?" Mrs. Goodman asked.

"I need a horse to pull logs off my property so I can turn it into farmland. But that's heavy work.

Maybe I need a draft horse."

Ordinarily, Rosalie would have leapt to her horse's defense. Major could do almost anything he set his mind to, and, she thought, he was just about as strong as any draft horse. But Rosalie didn't want to say anything that would encourage Mr. Green to buy Major. Rosalie glanced over at Major, hoping his feelings wouldn't be hurt that she hadn't stuck up for him. Major just gazed at her warmly.

"I'm going to need some time to make up my mind," said Mr. Green.

"Of course!" Rosalie said, quickly. "Take all the time you want."

Rosalie's mother gave her a stern look. "Go feed the cows," she said.

Rosalie knew she was being bold, but she was too desperate to care. Short of stealing Major and running away, she had to do everything in her power to keep anyone from buying him. Rosalie climbed the ladder into the hayloft and threw herself into a soft pile of hay. The pitchfork was leaning against the wall, but Rosalie didn't want to feed the cows. She didn't want to chop wood and shovel up manure and all the other backbreaking work Ed had always done. Maybe she *would* run away with Major. Let somebody else worry about the farm. She and Major would go find her father. Then everything would be all right.

First, of course, Rosalie would have to figure out where her father *was*. Sometimes his letters mentioned a battle or campsite, like Mount Jackson or Gettysburg, but his last letter didn't say anything at all about where he was. Rosalie pulled it out of her pocket. It was several months old and tattered around the edges. Rosalie had read it so many times that she had it memorized:

August 3, 1864

Dear Rosie,

Did my day perk up when I got your letter and the package you sent. I just about tore it open, hoping it was something good to eat, and it was! Cheddar cheese, gingerbread, and molasses cookies. You have no idea how delicious it all tasted, especially after the bad beef and spoiled bread they call food here. One of my buddies says the grub's so bad it's enough to make a mule desert and a hog wish he had never been born. Hard bread, bacon, and coffee is about all we draw.

I shared some of the cookies with Captain, who gobbled them right up. You asked how they were treating him, and let me set your mind to rest—the Union Army treats the horses better than the soldiers! Captain's got his own stall, fresh hay and water every day, and all the oats he can eat. He's in fine form. He's in good company, too, nothing but Morgans in this regiment, and a finer body of animals no one ever saw.

As for my regiment, there's true Yankee grit in every soldier. Never have we entered a battle where I haven't seen them fight to the finish and shed tears that they could not do more. Vermont forever! I am prouder than ever to be from this state, knowing the noble stand we Vermonters have taken in the great struggle.

But don't worry about your old dad. God has seen fit to protect me this far and I'm sure He'll watch over me still—none of those whizzing bullets has my name on it. I'll be home before you know it, watching over you while you do your lessons, making sure you don't try to slip away to see Major before your work is done.

How I long to see you again, and your brother and sister and mother, too. I wonder if I'll recognize you, you must have grown so since I saw you last. I hope you'll recognize me. I'm older and grayer, but I'm still and will always be,

Your loving father

Rosalie carefully refolded the letter, noting with worry that it was starting to tear along the creases. This was the last thing she had that her father had given her and it was starting to crumble. Maybe she should have kept it in her treasure box along with his other letters and her silver hairbrush. It would have been safer there than in her pocket.

And Rosalie knew she was only fooling herself about finding him. He could be anywhere—Virginia, Maryland, Pennsylvania . . . *lying wounded in the woods with nobody to help him.* No! Rosalie fought against the voice in her head putting her worst fears into words. *Maybe he was taken prisoner by the Confederates and he's starving or sick. Maybe he's dead . . .*

"No!" Rosalie shouted. She jumped up and grabbed the pitchfork. Jamming it under the hay, she pitched a shower of hay for the cows over the side of the loft and into the stable below.

CHAPTER FIVE

Rosalie's Idea

K*adiddly-dop, kadiddly-dop, kaddidly-dop.*

The smart rhythm of Major's hooves mixed with the clattering of the rickety wooden wagon that Rosalie drove into town a few days later. The wagon was laden with a load of cheddar cheese, dozens of hard, yellow rounds, each wrapped carefully in a piece of cloth. The Goodmans made the cheese in batches and aged it for months in a special shed. When the cheese was ready, they sold it to Eve Decker, owner of the general store in town, who then sold it to the people of Morrisville. Goodman Cheddar was known all over the county, and Rosalie knew they could have sold a lot more of it, but they'd lost so many cows they couldn't keep up with the demand.

Screeeeech-fump. Screeeeech-fump. Screeeeeech-fump.

Up ahead, coming around the curve from town, another wagon was inching slowly along. It was pulled by a horse so skinny and lame it was a wonder the wagon could move at all. Rosalie, covering the distance much faster, pulled up alongside the wagon and recognized Eve Decker and her old horse, Biscuit.

Eve was in her early twenties, slender and pale, with black hair twisted into a knot at the nape of her neck. Her dress and coat were black, too, because she was in mourning for her husband, Jeremy, who'd died a few years past in the war. He hadn't been shot in battle or anything glorious like that. He'd died of typhoid, a horrible illness. Many of the soldiers died of disease, Rosalie's father said, because the camps they lived in were dirty and filled with flies, mosquitoes, fleas, and lice.

Rosalie had felt terrible for Eve when her husband died. They'd only been married a few months and they'd just taken over running the General Store from Jeremy's father. Now Eve was running the store by herself.

"Eve!" Rosalie said in surprise. "I was just coming to see you. Where are you headed?"

"To Burlington, to pick up supplies," Eve said.

Burlington was the big city to the west of Morrisville. In good weather, it was less than a day's trip each way, but from the looks of Biscuit, Eve would be lucky if she made it there by tomorrow. And that was with the wagon *empty*. Rosalie wondered how such an old horse could possibly pull the wagon full of supplies. In fact, Rosalie was almost certain it couldn't.

Unfortunately, Eve, like everyone else around here, didn't have much choice. Good horses were hard to find because of the war. Wasn't that what everyone was always saying? Rosalie was sure her mother would find lots of buyers for Major, once word got out that he was for sale. Too bad she couldn't just lend a little bit of him to everybody.

Rosalie's brow wrinkled. An idea was starting to form in the back of her mind.

"Don't look so worried, Rosalie," Eve said. "You can still drop off your cheese. My sister's minding the store."

"No, no," Rosalie said. "I wasn't worried about that. I was just thinking." The idea was clearer now, and so natural that Rosalie couldn't believe she hadn't thought of it before. It was the perfect solution to all her problems. "Eve," Rosalie said. "Do you really think Biscuit's going to make it all the way to Burlington and then all the way back?"

Eve sighed. "What choice do I have? We're almost out of salt and coffee, and I've got to pick up a mower I ordered for Mr. Bober. This can't wait, Rosalie."

"I wasn't criticizing," Rosalie said. "But why don't you rent a stronger horse to take you to Burlington?"

Eve laughed. "Every horse in town is so overworked, I'm sure no one can spare one. But thank you for thinking of me." Eve slapped her reins against Biscuit's back, and the horse tiredly started walking again.

"Wait, Eve!" Rosalie called out. "You can rent Major."

"Whoa!" Eve pulled on Biscuit's reins, though it was hardly necessary. Biscuit hadn't gone more than a few feet. "How much?" Eve asked Rosalie.

Rosalie didn't know what to answer. She'd never set a price for anything. "Uh, let's see," Rosalie said, stalling. "You can have him 'til tomorrow morning and I'll charge you. . . one dollar."

Eve bit her lip. "That's kind of high . . ."

Rosalie wanted to kick herself. She'd come so close to making some much-needed money and she'd ruined everything by being too greedy.

". . . but it beats breaking down somewhere along the way," Eve said. "You've got yourself a deal."

"I'll even take Biscuit home," Rosalie offered. "I was on my way to your place anyway. I'll hitch him up to my wagon."

Eve did something Rosalie hadn't seen her do in months. She smiled. "You've thought of everything!" she said admiringly. Hopping down off her wagon, she unhitched Biscuit while Rosalie did the same with Major.

Rosalie patted Major on the neck. "You be a good boy, now," she said. "I'll see you tomorrow."

Major leaned forward and nuzzled Rosalie's cheek. Then he allowed Eve to lead him to her wagon. After the horses had been rehitched, Rosalie watched Major as he briskly trotted down the road pulling Eve's wagon. He looked so strong and capable and confident. Rosalie was sure Eve would have no problem filling her orders and getting back in good time. But now Rosalie had a problem. A big problem. How was she going to explain herself when she arrived home without Major and without the wagon?

"You did *what???*" Rosalie's mother said in amazement a few hours later. She stood in the barn looking at Morgan's empty stall.

"I rented him," Rosalie said with a lot more confidence than she felt. "He's earning a whole dollar!

And we'll have him back tomorrow."

"What about the herd?" Rachel Goodman asked. "Who's going to drive them in from the pasture this evening? Or hadn't you thought of that."

"I had!" Rosalie fibbed. "I can bring them in. I'll just use a switch. Most of them come in on their own anyway." *Except Clarence and Homer*, Rosalie added to herself.

Without another word, Rosalie's mother strode from the barn and headed for the house. Rosalie scurried after her.

"Please, Mama," she begged. "Don't be angry. We can use the money, can't we? And when. . . *if* you sell Major, we wouldn't have him around to herd the cattle anyway."

Rachel Goodman kept walking without slowing her pace. "Clean out the stables," she called over her shoulder as she pulled open the kitchen door.

Rosalie stood on the hard, bare earth and watched her mother disappear into the house. Rosalie hadn't thought her mother would be happy she'd rented out Major without asking, but she'd expected her to come around eventually. She'd thought she could warm her mother up to the idea of renting Major out to more people in need of horses. But from the way her mother was acting, Rosalie didn't see much chance of that.

Rosalie turned and trudged slowly toward the barn. The hope she'd felt just a few hours ago was fading away to nothing. Rosalie pulled on an old frock coat and grabbed a shovel so she could start cleaning out the cow manure piled in the stables.

The next afternoon, as Rosalie was emptying a pan full of water into the yard, she heard a familiar sound.

Kadiddly-dop, kadiddly-dop, kaddidly-dop, kaddidly-dop.

Rosalie looked up and saw Major pulling Eve Decker's wagon. The wagon was filled to bursting with wooden crates and barrels of rice, salt, and coffee, bolts of cloth, bags of flour, new brooms and mops, feed sacks, and a large contraption that looked like a tricycle with a long rake attached. Despite the heavy load, Major was stepping lively. Eve, too, looked refreshed despite the long drive back from Burlington. It was the first time in a long time Rosalie had seen Eve without dark circles under her eyes.

Rosalie dropped the tin pan and ran toward the road. Major stopped when he saw her coming and whinnied happily. "I missed you," Rosalie whispered into his soft coat as she hugged him around the neck. She reached into her pocket to see if she had anything sweet to give him, but her pockets were empty.

"He's some horse," Eve said, jumping down off the wagon and coming alongside Rosalie. "He didn't need to stop and rest and even let me saddle him up last night to go for a ride around Burlington. Of course, he did sweet talk me into buying these." Eve pulled a sugar cookie out of a brown paper bag and held it out to Major. His lips quickly covered the cookie and made it disappear.

"Major's very tricky that way," Rosalie agreed. "He knows just what to do to talk you out of a sugar cookie."

Eve laughed and scratched the top of Major's head. "Rosalie," she said thoughtfully, "I was wondering. Do you think you might let me borrow Major once a week for my trips into Burlington? I'd pay you a dollar each time."

Rosalie quickly added some numbers in her head. One dollar a week meant four dollars a month, still not enough to pay the mortgage, but a big help. Rosalie was afraid to bring up the subject of renting Major again, but she couldn't let this opportunity pass by. "I'll ask my mother," Rosalie promised.

"Fine," Eve said, hopping back up on the wagon. "After I unload my wagon, I'll bring Major right back."

As Eve and Major rode away, Rosalie saw Eve

wave into the distance. Rosalie couldn't see whom Eve was waving at, but figured it either had to be a passing wagon or someone walking on the road. As Eve's wagon got a little further away, Rosalie saw that there was someone walking—a tall, heavyset man with a beard and a dark hat.

Rosalie's heart started thumping. She knew who that man was, and she had a pretty good guess where he was heading. Rosalie stood frozen to the ground as Joseph Green approached. He stopped when he reached her and took off his hat. "Good day, Rosalie," he said politely. "Is your mother at home?"

Rosalie simply nodded. She was afraid that if she opened her mouth to speak, her heart would jump right out of her mouth.

"I suppose you know why I've come," he said, almost apologetically. Rosalie closed her eyes and waited for the words she'd hoped she'd never hear. "I want to buy Major."

Rosalie Strikes a Deal

"Mr. Green!" Rosalie's mother greeted her neighbor with a smile as she wiped her wet hands on her apron. "Please come in."

Joseph Green took off his hat and bowed his head slightly as he ducked under the doorway leading into the kitchen. "I hope I've come at a good time," he said.

"Of course!" Rachel Goodman said, lifting a pot off the stove and grabbing a mug from the shelf. "Won't you have some coffee?"

Rosalie, standing in the doorway, wanted to scream. How could the two of them act so friendly and polite when they were about to ruin her life?

"Thank you," Mr. Green said, taking the steaming cup. "Looks like we're in for some rain."

"The almanac predicted a solid week of rain," Rosalie's mother agreed, taking a ceramic bowl filled with fresh-baked biscuits and placing it on the table in front of her guest. Mr. Green took a biscuit and bit into it.

Rosalie could hardly stand it. If they were going to talk about selling Major, why didn't they get it over with? Were they trying to torture her on purpose?

Mr. Green brushed some crumbs out of his beard. Then he cleared his throat. "Uh, Mrs. Goodman," he said, "I suppose you know why I've come. I'm prepared to offer you a good price for your Morgan horse. A fair price."

Rosalie slipped inside the kitchen and wedged herself between the sink and the cupboard, trying to make herself as small as possible. Mrs. Goodman didn't answer Mr. Green. She just waited for him to continue.

"The sum I am offering," Mr. Green said, "is fifty dollars."

Mrs. Goodman gasped. "Fifty dollars? Major's worth a lot more than that. I was expecting you to say *one hundred* and fifty."

Mr. Green laughed. "Why, ma'am, if I were made of money, I'd gladly give it to you. But I'm just a farmer like yourself, with a mortgage of my own to pay off. I won't see any money coming in until next year's harvest. And your horse is pretty small. But I may be able to scrape up a little more. What about sixty dollars?"

Rachel Goodman bit her lip. Rosalie knew her mother was doing some arithmetic in her head. Sixty dollars would pay a few months' mortgage and some expenses. "I don't know," Rachel said, shaking her head. "Once that money's gone, I'm right back where I started, and I won't even have a horse. On the other hand, . . ." Rachel turned to Rosalie and almost looked as if she were about to ask for Rosalie's opinion on the matter.

Rosalie knew she was taking a big risk, but this might be the only chance she'd have to tell her mother her idea. "Mama, why don't you *rent* Major to Mr. Green?" she asked. "Instead of selling him."

Rosalie's mother and Mr. Green looked at Rosalie as if she were speaking a foreign language. But at least they hadn't said no yet. Rosalie kept going.

"You see, the way I figure," she said, "you'd *both* end up saving money. Mr. Green can pay us some money every week to rent Major, but it wouldn't cost him as much as buying Major. And we'd still get to keep him! You said yourself, Mama, that he's worth a lot more than Mr. Green has offered."

Rosalie's mother found her voice. She turned to Mr. Green. "I have to apologize for my daughter," she said. "She's not usually this outspoken . . ."

Mr. Green waved away her words with his hand. "No need to apologize, Mrs. Goodman. Your daughter may have a point."

Rosalie clutched her fists to her chest. Was it possible, just possible, that Mr. Green might see it her way?

Mr. Green took a long, noisy sip of coffee, then put his mug down on the table. "I never considered renting a horse," he said slowly, "but it might make good financial sense. I really only need a horse in the short term to pull the logs off my property. Then I can do without one until spring. By then, who knows? The war may be over and I may be able to get a horse cheap. Or even a pair of oxen to pull my plow." Mr. Green turned to look at Rosalie. "How much?" he asked. "How much would you charge me to rent your horse?"

Rosalie's mother looked at her, too, with an amazed look on her face. Suddenly Rachel wasn't the only one making decisions. All the responsibility was making Rosalie nervous, but she knew she had to come up with an answer. Eve Decker had been willing to pay a dollar for Major, but that was overnight, and that was hauling all the way to Burlington and back.

"Sixty cents a day," Rosalie said firmly. "You can have him five days a week. But Eve Decker gets him on Monday and Tuesday."

"I don't know," Mr. Green said. "That seems kind of high for such a *small* horse . . ."

Now that Rosalie had been through this with Eve, she had a lot more confidence. "Well," she said, "logging is really tough work. You're not going to find a horse as strong or as smart as Major anywhere around. And if you don't want him, there's plenty of other people in town who will!"

Rachel Goodman was about to say something to Mr. Green, probably another apology about Rosalie's sassy mouth. But Mr. Green spoke first.

"It's a deal," he told Rosalie, with no small amount of admiration in his voice. "You're one hard bargainer."

Rosalie turned with pride to her mother. "Major will be earning four dollars a week," she said. "That's more than sixteen dollars a month. Between that and the money we make from our butter and cheese, won't we be able to pay the mortgage now?"

Rachel Goodman's mouth hung open in disbelief. She shut it quickly and turned to Mr. Green. "When do you want Major to start work?"

"How about Wednesday morning?" Mr. Green said.

Saturday morning, Rosalie opened her eyes and stared around her darkened bedroom. Everything was soft and gray and fuzzy—the washstand over in the corner, her dresses and Mathilda's smaller ones hanging on pegs against the wall, and the tiny, straight-back chair her father had made for her when she was little. It was hard to tell from the light what time it was, but Rosalie guessed it was early morning. If it were sunny, it would have been a lot easier to tell, but the sun hadn't shown itself for over a week.

Just as the almanac had predicted, they'd had nothing but rain. Major hadn't been able to start his job with Mr. Green yet and Eve had canceled her trip into Burlington, too. Even though Major's jobs had been put off, Rosalie knew the bank's mortgage payment couldn't be. If Major didn't start work soon, Rosalie's family would be in trouble all over again.

Rosalie hopped out of bed and ran across the cold wooden floor. Shivering, she looked out the window. Broken tree branches lay scattered over the muddy fields. But the sky, while gray, showed no immediate signs of opening up with another downpour.

Rosalie ran to her washstand and quickly splashed some water on her face. This was Major's first day of work with Mr. Green, and she didn't want to be late!

"I hope you'll forgive me for making you work so hard," Rosalie said to Major in his stall a few minutes later, "but it was the only choice I had. And at least you get to come home with me every night."

Major didn't answer. He was too busy eating the special hot breakfast Rosalie had made for him this morning, bran mash with hot water and molasses. Rosalie was massaging Major with a curry comb to loosen up the dirt under his coat.

"And you may get really tired," Rosalie warned. "Logs can be heavy to pull. But you're strong. I know you can do it."

Major tossed back his head and snorted, as if to say "Of course I can!"

Rosalie picked up Major's dandy brush and started going over his back and sides with short, quick strokes. Before long, Major's brown coat was gleaming. "You're going to look so handsome when Mr. Green sees you," she said proudly. "Let him try to say you're just a small horse. We'll show him you're stronger than anybody."

Major stamped his hoof and tried to nudge open the stall door with his nose.

"All right, all right," Rosalie said, laughing. "I know you can't wait to show him what you've got. Let's go!"

"Where is it?" Cassie asked Rosalie a little later, as the two rode Major up a steeply sloping, rocky road. Cassie had wanted to come with Rosalie to Mr. Green's this morning so she could wish Major luck with his new job. Rosalie was grateful her friend was coming along. Though Rosalie had bargained with Mr. Green like a grown-up, she had been a little nervous about taking Major to his farm all by herself.

"He said it was to the right after the fork in the road," Rosalie said, trying to peer through the bare trees for some sign of a field or farmhouse. All she saw were more trees. There was a distant, whooshing sound which Rosalie recognized as the rushing of the Lamoille River. Major stepped gingerly over a fallen tree and splashed through a giant puddle.

Cassie pointed into the distance. "There!" she cried. "I think I see something."

Rosalie looked and saw a little cabin in the woods. It was just a one-room cabin with a roof of split logs and a window covered with wooden shutters. Rosalie urged Major on, but she was confused. This didn't look like a farmhouse or a farm.

As the girls approached, Mr. Green came out of the cabin. He was wearing the same dark coat and hat he'd worn every other time Rosalie had seen him.

"Hello!" he said and waved at them. A woman appeared behind him, small and slight with wispy blond hair. She, too, waved. Rosalie guessed this must be Mrs. Green.

"Welcome to our farm!" Mr. Green said, laughing. "I know it doesn't look like much yet, but that's why you're here."

"Would you girls like some breakfast?" Mrs. Green asked. "I've got some fried eggs, fried potatoes, and a huge pot of oatmeal simmering."

It all sounded delicious, but Rosalie had already eaten and she couldn't stay. "Thank you," Rosalie said, "but I've got to get right back home to start my chores."

Mr. Green rubbed his large, rough hands together. "Then let's go!" he said excitedly. "Let's make a farm!"

Mr. Green walked a little way through the woods and the girls followed. He led them through a thicket of evergreen trees and stopped. The girls gazed at what looked like a swamp studded with logs.

Mr. Green turned around and smiled. "Doesn't look like much, does it?"

Rosalie didn't know what to answer. Her eyes ran over the sloping muddy ground covered with all those stumps and logs and her heart sank. How on earth was Major going to be able to clear all this land all by himself? The girls dismounted, and Rosalie patted Major comfortingly.

"Our job's a lot tougher now because of the rain," Mr. Green admitted. "The Lamoille overflowed and these logs are pretty well stuck." He studied Rosalie's face, which, she knew, must have a horrified look on it. "You're not thinking of backing out?" he asked, looking worried.

Rosalie looked at her horse. "That's up to Major," she said.

Major, too, looked over the property, though it was hard to tell what he thought of it.

Mr. Green glanced over Rosalie's head and waved.

Rosalie turned and saw a young man leading an enormous draft horse through the evergreen trees. The horse's coat was gray speckled with white, and it looked to be at least seventeen hands high. Its back and neck were huge and round, and its legs were as thick as tree stumps. It must have weighed at least a ton! As it came up alongside them, Major suddenly looked tiny and fragile.

"What kind of horse is that?" Rosalie asked,

looking up at its massive head.

"Percheron," the young man answered. "Though he's more of a mountain than a horse," he added with pride in his voice.

The Percheron snorted at Major, and its ears flattened against the back of its head. Major's eyes widened and his nostrils flared.

"Uh-oh," Cassie whispered to Rosalie. "It doesn't look as though the two of them are going to be friends."

"This is Cal Buckwald and Johnny Boy," Mr. Green said, introducing the man and his horse. "Rosalie, I liked your idea of renting so much that I decided to rent two horses to make the work go faster!"

Cal nodded at the girls and then looked at the fallen trees scattered all over the field. "Johnny can get those out," he said confidently. "Johnny logged twenty acres last year, over at the Hanson place."

Rosalie glanced nervously at Cassie. Major had never done any logging in his entire life. And he was half the size of Johnny Boy. Rosalie hadn't counted on this at all. With two horses, there'd only be half as much work for Major, which meant half as much money. And what if Johnny Boy worked harder and faster than Major? Maybe Major would lose his job altogether!

Mr. Green clapped his hands together. "Okay, everybody," he said. "Let's get to work!"

CHAPTER SEVEN

A Hard Day's Work

Mr. Green put the work collar over the horses' heads. Then he hooked some long chains onto the collars. "We'll wrap these chains around each log," he said, pointing, "and pull them up to the top of that rise over there. The Lamoille's just below. That way, come spring, I can float the logs downstream and sell them for lumber."

Cal Buckwald nodded. "You could get a good price for some of this wood."

Rosalie nodded, too, though she didn't really know what the two men were talking about.

"The tough part," said Mr. Green, "is going to be wrapping the chains around the logs."

"What about wedges to lift 'em up?" Cal asked. "Or roll the logs over the chain to get it around."

Mr. Green shook his head. "Mud's too thick. Those logs don't want to go anywhere."

Cal frowned, but he led Johnny Boy into the mud toward a nearby log. Rosalie followed with Major. The mud swallowed up their boots and hooves and didn't want to let go.

"*Ee-ee-ee-ee!*" Johnny Boy complained, tossing his head back. Being so big and heavy, he sank more deeply into the mud than anyone else.

"Come on, Johnny Boy," Cal encouraged him, trying to lead him to a rocky place where the mud wasn't so thick.

With an angry snort, Johnny Boy heaved one enormous leg out of the mud and pulled himself up onto the rock. Major, too, was having trouble, but he found it easier to pick his way from one dry spot to another because he was smaller and lighter.

Mr. Green picked up the chains attached to Johnny Boy and wrapped them around the stumps of branches on the end of a log. "There," he said when he'd tightened up the chains. "That should give you something to pull against." Mr. Green hooked up Major to another log. Rosalie noticed that the log he'd chosen for Major was shorter, and not as thick.

Rosalie knew what that meant. It meant Mr. Green didn't think Major was as strong or as useful as Johnny Boy.

Cal slapped Johnny Boy's hindquarters. "Come on, Boy!" he shouted.

Johnny Boy planted his enormous hooves and pulled against the chains as he tried to move forward. The log quivered in the mud but held fast. Grunting from the strain, Johnny Boy managed to move the log a few inches.

"Atta boy, Johnny!" Cal encouraged him, as the Percheron continued moving forward.

Rosalie whispered in Major's ear. "You can do it." She patted his hindquarters.

Major lowered his head and leaned forward. The chains tightened and stretched between the horse and the log. Major shifted his weight to the right, causing the log to roll slightly. Then Major shifted left, loosening the log a little more.

"Good thinking, Major!" Rosalie said. Major may not have the strength and weight of a draft horse, but his intelligence more than made up for it.

Major kept rocking until the log loosened, then he gave one tremendous heave. The log lurched free. Gaining momentum, Major picked his way carefully through the mud, trying to step in the drier places.

Johnny Boy had also managed to pull his log forward, but he was having a harder time getting through the mud. Everywhere he stepped, his tremendous weight caused him to sink. His tail swished and he bared his teeth as he strained and grunted. Cal leaned over in the mud and tried to lift Johnny Boy's legs for him, to help him get free. Johnny Boy seemed to understand that Cal was trying to help him, because he stood still, letting Cal do the work. Cal struggled, but was unable to lift the leg.

Meanwhile, Major had reached the top of the rise, where he waited patiently.

"Better get that log unhooked," Mr. Green said to Cal, as he slogged through the mud toward Major.

Cal waded around behind Johnny Boy and unhooked the log. Johnny stepped sideways, freeing himself, then turned around. He headed slowly for the evergreen trees.

"Hey!" Mr. Green shouted at the Percheron. "You're going the wrong way!"

"No," Cassie whispered to Rosalie. "Johnny Boy knows exactly where he's going. Home."

That seemed to be just what the draft horse had in mind.

"Come back here!" Cal shouted, running after the horse, or at least trying to, as the mud kept grabbing his feet.

Johnny Boy waited long enough for Cal to catch up. Then the draft horse ran down the hill as fast as he could, with Cal right behind.

"Well," Mr. Green said after they'd disappeared, "I guess that just leaves Major."

Rosalie and Cassie looked at Major, who was nibbling at the few remaining leaves on the low branch of a nearby tree. He seemed completely unconcerned that he'd just shown up a horse twice his size. But Rosalie couldn't have been prouder. She was relieved, too, that Major was the only horse who could do the job. That guaranteed him work for at least a few months.

"I guess we'd better be getting home," Rosalie told Mr. Green. "I'll be back later to pick up Major."

"I'll take good care of him," Mr. Green said. Then he led him down the slope. "Are you ready for another log?" Mr. Green asked the Morgan.

That afternoon, when Rosalie returned, the first thing she saw was a huge pile of logs at the top of the rise. There had to be two dozen of them, at least. Rosalie looked around for Major and Mr. Green but didn't see either one of them. Rosalie grew worried. Had Major collapsed from exhaustion after hauling so many tons of wood?

"Hellooooooo!" Rosalie called through the trees. "Anybody here?"

There was no answer.

"Major!" Rosalie called, really worried now.

Major emerged from the trees, Mr. Green by his side, hauling a crude wooden sled loaded with tree stumps. The tree stumps were covered with thick brown mud and their roots dangled in every direction. Major whinnied happily when he saw Rosalie, and he picked up the pace. The mud seemed to have dried out some since the morning and the going was a little easier.

"How did he do?" Rosalie asked Mr. Green, though she could already guess.

Mr. Green patted Major fondly. "He's a hard worker," he answered. "And he really is worth a hundred fifty dollars. I just wish I had the money to pay it."

And I'm glad you don't, Rosalie thought with relief. "I'm here to take him home now," she said. "But I'll bring him back bright and early tomorrow."

"Here's his pay," Mr. Green said, handing Rosalie sixty cents.

Major nosed at the side pocket of Mr. Green's coat.

"Hey!" Mr. Green said. "What do you think you're doing?"

With great delicacy, Major lifted a large sugar cookie out of Mr. Green's pocket.

"How'd that get in there?" Mr. Green asked. He was acting surprised, but Rosalie knew he was joking. She'd seen Major work his charms on too many people.

After Major had finished his treat, Rosalie hopped on his back. "Let's go home," she said. "I'm gonna give you a rubdown and a nice bran mash. You deserve it!"

Rosalie rode Major off Mr. Green's property and back down the rocky road. A whooshing sound in the distance caught Rosalie's attention. She thought it must be the swollen Lamoille, rushing down its riverbed. But there was hollering, too. Human voices. Young, male voices. Major's ears pricked up and he began to trot down the road.

"Go get 'im, Babe!" a voice shouted.

"Come on, Mistletoe!" called someone else.

As Rosalie and Major reached the fork, they saw what the excitement was all about. Two horses, with a boy mounted bareback on each one, were running up the road at breakneck speed, heading straight toward them!

The Race

Rosalie pulled on Major's reins, and he dodged to the right, just barely avoiding the two horses. There was a rush of air and a hurtling of hooves as they raced past. Rosalie turned Major so she could watch. One horse was a ruddy brown Thoroughbred and the other a Quarter Racing Horse, a blue roan, which meant his coat was black with sprinklings of white. Both were breathing hard and lathered with sweat. They were running side by side, but the Quarter Horse was slowly inching forward. Just ahead of them, Rosalie noticed a tree branch with a white handkerchief hanging off it. Rosalie guessed this must be the finish line.

Her guess was correct because as soon as the Quarter Horse passed it, some of the boys watching the race cheered. "Hooray, Mistletoe!" they shouted. Most of the boys who watched were sitting astride horses of their own.

Mistletoe's rider, a stocky boy with hair as black as his horse's, held an outstretched palm to the boy atop the Thoroughbred. "Pay up," he demanded.

The Thoroughbred's rider, looking none too pleased, pulled a dollar out of his pocket and handed it over. "That's my whole day's pay," he complained. "My daddy's gonna tan my hide when he finds out."

"So don't tell him!" another boy shouted, laughing as if he'd said something really funny.

Mistletoe's rider raised the money high above his head. "Who dares to challenge the fastest horse on earth?" he shouted.

There was a respectful silence. Then Major stepped toward the Quarter Horse as if he were responding to the challenge. He pawed the ground and whinnied.

One of the other boys on horseback laughed and pointed. "Look at that little Morgan!" he sneered. "Does he think he's a racing horse?"

"Looks more like a pony," another joked.

Rosalie felt her face get hot despite the chilly

wind. "Don't you dare talk about my horse that way!" she shouted. "He's plenty fast!"

"Oh, yeah?" Mistletoe's rider asked. "You want to bet some money on that?"

Rosalie fingered the coins in her pocket, the money Major had just earned at Mr. Green's. If Major won the race, he could double that money in just a few minutes. Wouldn't her mother be pleased to see a dollar and twenty cents instead of just sixty?

Rosalie studied the Quarter Horse. It looked to be about fifteen hands high, not much taller than Major, but much more powerful. It had a white star on its forehead and white socks on its hind legs. Though it was winded and sweaty, it looked ready for another race.

Major, on the other hand, had spent the last eight hours doing backbreaking work, and his hooves were caked with dried mud. He wasn't exactly in top form. And Rosalie didn't want to risk losing all the money he'd worked so hard to earn.

"I don't know," Rosalie said, wondering if there was a graceful way out of this.

"What's the matter?" Mistletoe's rider taunted. "You scared? Or maybe your horse is."

Major's ears flattened against his head and his neck stretched out toward Mistletoe. Then he stomped his feet. It was clear Major wasn't scared. He was ready to race. Rosalie's mind was made up. She couldn't stand in the way of Major's honor.

Rosalie pulled the sixty cents out of her pocket and showed it to the boy. "This is all I've got," she said. "Is it enough?"

The boy shrugged. "It'll do. I'll match it. Winner take all."

Though Rosalie was now trembling with anxiety, she tried to keep her voice steady. "Winner take all," she agreed.

"I'll show you the starting line," the boy said. He squeezed his calves together, and Mistletoe trotted back down the rutted road. Rosalie followed on Major. As they passed, the other boys cheered and jeered. Some of them were also showing each other money, placing bets of their own.

Major and Mistletoe took their places beside each other behind a crude line drawn with a stick in the mud. A small boy in an overcoat that was too big for him drew a red bandanna from inside his overlong sleeve.

"On your marks!" the boy shouted. "Get set . . ."

The boy raised the red bandanna over his head.

Rosalie's body was poised and taut. Major, too, was tight and quivering.

The boy lowered the red bandanna in a sweeping motion. "Go!"

Major burst forward, as fresh and lively as if he'd just woken up from a nice long nap. Rosalie felt as if she could barely control such power, so she just let him run. She was aware of Mistletoe right beside them, inches away, his coat shiny with sweat. His whole body stretched forward as if he were trying to fly more than run. His hooves churned up clods of mud and dirt as he darted ahead of Major. Rosalie wanted to cry. Though Major was fast and strong, he wasn't bred for running the way a Quarter Horse was.

But Major wasn't finished yet. He pushed himself to go a little faster.

"Yeah, Major!" Rosalie urged him on.

Major inched up on Mistletoe until they were dead even. Rosalie caught a quick glimpse of Mistletoe's rider, who was pressed flat against his horse's neck. The two of them seemed fused, as if one being. The rider seemed to be saying something in his horse's ear. Rosalie couldn't hear over the clatter of hooves, but Mistletoe seemed to. Though he'd seemed to be giving everything he had, he somehow found a little bit more. Mistletoe edged forward again as they neared the finish line.

The white handkerchief hanging off the branch

was now only a few yards away and Mistletoe's lead was lengthening. Rosalie clutched her horse's neck in despair. It looked as if it were all over. She'd lost everything—the race and, even worse, the money she was supposed to give her mother.

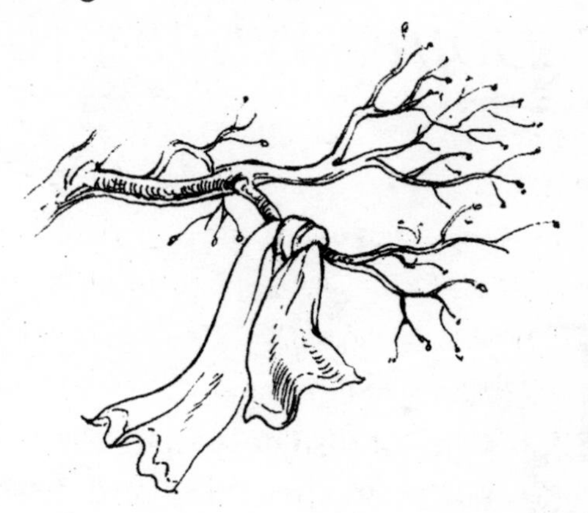

Doing What's Right

The sight of Mistletoe's retreating backside caused Major to do something he'd never done before. He roared. Or, at least, it sounded like a roar. It was a low, powerful sound that came from somewhere deep inside him, reverberating in Rosalie's bones. The sound seemed to propel Major forward, like a gust of wind behind him, pushing him past Mistletoe and past the white handkerchief. Major won by less than a nose!

A few of the boys whooped and hollered, no doubt the ones who'd been brave enough to bet on Major. Even the ones who were handing over their money looked on the Morgan with grudging admiration.

The boy on Mistletoe reached into his pocket and handed Rosalie sixty cents. "You won fair and square," he said. "I don't know how you did it on that little horse, though."

"Maybe he's got wings!" said the boy astride Babe, the Thoroughbred.

"He's got *spirit*," Rosalie said, leaning down to pat her horse's sweaty neck. "And that more than makes up for anything else."

Rosalie put the boy's sixty cents together with the money from her pocket. The silver coins glowed pink in the waning afternoon light. One dollar and twenty cents. It was amazing how quickly the second sixty cents had been won. In less than two minutes, Major had earned the same amount it had taken him eight hours to earn pulling logs. Maybe there was something to this racing thing. At this rate, Major could earn a lot more than four dollars a week. Rosalie couldn't wait to tell her mother what had happened.

"You did *what?*" Rosalie's mother said, glaring at her over the potatoes she was peeling for dinner.

"I raced him," Rosalie said, the money still sitting in her outstretched hand. "We doubled our money in no time! And Mama, you should have seen him on the final stretch. It was as if some magical force took over and pushed us across the finish line. One of the boys said Major had wings! Come on, Mama. Take the money."

Rachel Goodman merely glared at the coins in Rosalie's hand. "I wouldn't even touch it," she said angrily. "Don't you realize what you were doing? You were *gambling*! Gambling with money we need to keep a roof over our heads!"

"I know that," Rosalie admitted. "And I know it's wrong, but I really didn't have any choice."

"Of course you did," her mother objected. "You always have a choice."

"But they were teasing him," Rosalie said, tears springing to her eyes. "They were making fun of him because he's small. And Major's the one who wanted to race, not me."

Rachel tilted her head down and looked at Rosalie through half-lowered eyelids. "You're trying to blame this on a *horse*?"

Even though Rosalie had been telling the truth, she knew what her mother was getting at. Major was just an animal. Rosalie was a human being who was responsible both for herself and for him. And she had no right to risk injuring her horse who worked so hard for her. Rosalie suddenly felt ashamed. "I'm sorry," she said in a small voice. "I promise I'll never do it again."

"That's not good enough," her mother said, taking a large knife and cutting one of the potatoes into thick slices. "I want you to give that boy back his money."

"Give it back?" Rosalie cried, lowering her hand which still held all the money. "Why should I do that?"

Rachel reached for another potato and began cutting it, too. "Because," she said, "it's the right thing to do."

"But he would have kept the money if *he'd* won the race," Rosalie insisted.

"It doesn't matter," her mother said. "Just because other people are wrong doesn't give you an excuse to be. I didn't raise my daughter to be a gambler."

Rosalie tried one last plea. "I don't know the boy's name," she said. "How will I even find him?"

"You'll find him," her mother said with certainty. "You're smart enough at figuring out everything else." Rachel gave her daughter a softer look. Rosalie knew she would be forgiven when the money was returned. Rosalie carefully counted out sixty cents and held it out to her mother. "Here," she said. "That's what Major earned honestly. We can keep that, can't we?"

Rachel didn't look up from her potatoes. "Leave it on the table," she instructed.

As Rosalie rode Major back down the road looking for the boys, she thought about what her mother had said. Rosalie could see why her mother thought gambling was wrong, and Rosalie felt badly about what she'd done. But she couldn't help feeling proud of her horse. Major could work harder and longer than any draft horse and *still* outrace a bigger horse, all in the same day!

At Long Last

Rosalie inhaled deeply as she walked up the steep, rocky road. Though her boots were crunching through snow, the air smelled sweet and damp. It was early April, and spring, while not there yet, had sent a warm breeze to tell everyone it was on its way. Melting ice dripped from the branches of maple trees, and tiny crocuses were starting to push their delicate heads through the damp earth.

Bearing right at the fork in the road, Rosalie noticed a new spring that had appeared overnight, trickling amidst the trees. A raccoon, drinking from the spring, paused to glance at Rosalie through its black furry mask.

Up ahead, through the still-bare branches, Rosalie could see the Greens' house. It was a lot larger than it had been the first time she saw it. Some of the logs Major had pulled off the property had become walls, and split timbers formed its sloping roof. Inside there were three real rooms now, a kitchen, a bedroom, and a tiny parlor that was Mrs. Green's pride and joy. She'd already filled it with pretty chairs and a sofa she'd brought from their last house and often invited Rosalie in for tea while Rosalie was waiting for Major to finish his work.

Mrs. Green appeared at the door now, waving as Rosalie approached the house. She was in her fourth month of pregnancy, and her cheeks were round and rosy. "Come on in!" she invited Rosalie. "I've made some gingerbread."

"I'd love some," Rosalie said, "but I can't stay today. I've got to get Major home so Mr. Bober can take a look at him. He may want to breed Major with his mare, and he's willing to pay ten dollars!"

Mrs. Green smiled. "Major's earning quite a lot of money for you."

"I know," Rosalie said proudly. "He's got more work than he can handle. He's going to help the McWalters with their sugaring next week, and the week after that he's driving Ethan Jones up to

Montpelier to visit his aunt and uncle."

Mrs. Green shook her head, impressed. "Guess your mother won't have any trouble making the mortgage payments now."

"It looks good right now," Rosalie said. "We were able to hire Ed back, and we're going to rent a team of oxen for the spring planting so Major can work at his other jobs. I'll even get to go back to school!"

Mrs. Green wrapped her arms around Rosalie and squeezed her tight. "That's so good to hear," she said. Then she winked. "I know how much you missed your teacher, Nasty Nellie."

"*Nelson*," Rosalie corrected her with a laugh. Mrs. Green was always making up other names for Miss Nelson, like Nasty Nancy and Mean Margaret. "Well, I'd better get Major," she told the farmer's wife.

"Here," Mrs. Green said, darting back into the house and reappearing with a plate of gingerbread cookies. Rosalie laughed when she saw the shape of the cookies. Each one looked like a little brown horse. "For Major's last day," Mrs. Green said with a smile.

Rosalie took two, one for herself, and one for her horse. "Thank you," she said, skipping toward the pine trees that led toward the farm.

Emerging on the other side, Rosalie couldn't help but smile when she saw the broad sloping field. While it was still rocky in places, it was completely free of trees or tree stumps. In another week or two, Mr. Green could start plowing.

Mr. Green appeared from some distant trees with Major beside him. Even at this distance, Major recognized Rosalie right away and whinnied. Rosalie hid the gingerbread cookie in the pocket of her coat and waited for him to approach.

When Major reached her, he went straight for her pocket and snatched the cookie right out.

"Well!" Rosalie said, pretending to be hurt. "I'm happy to see you, too!"

Major seemed to understand the joke because he pushed his nose playfully into Rosalie's chest. She reached up to scratch between his ears.

Mr. Green sighed. "I'm really going to miss this little horse," he said. "I've gotten so used to seeing him every day that I don't know what I'll do when he's gone."

"You can always come visit us," Rosalie promised. "And we'll come see you, too."

"You'd better," Mr. Green said. He leaned over and kissed Major's nose. "Good-bye, my friend," he said.

Major nickered softly as if he, too, were saying good-bye.

Mr. Green boosted Rosalie up onto Major's back,

and she rode up the rise toward the road. The Lamoille River was visible in the valley below, its water rushing and pushing as if it were in a big hurry to get somewhere. As Major picked his way over knotted tree roots and fallen branches, Rosalie felt peaceful inside. Her life was so much better than it had been only a few months ago. It was such a relief to not have to worry about losing the farm, and she was even looking forward to seeing her teacher again.

But even though things were better, Rosalie never felt quite right. She still felt empty inside, as if she were just marking time and waiting.

As they approached the road, Major's ears pricked up and his nostrils flared. He moved quickly through the trees and onto the road. Rosalie looked behind her, wondering if they were being followed.

"What's the matter?" Rosalie asked her horse.

Major began to trot. His head strained forward as if he were reaching for something.

"Major?" Rosalie asked, completely befuddled.

When Major reached the fork in the road, he paused for a moment, looked around, then began to run in the direction of the farm. Rosalie looked around, too, but she didn't see anything. Then Major stopped abruptly and stared into the distance.

Rosalie finally saw what Major was staring at. It

was a horse, far off in the distance, stepping slowly and carefully. Major started to quiver, and he whinnied happily. Rosalie, too, felt a strange excitement. She recognized the lines of that horse. It was a Morgan! A dark chestnut Morgan with a clean-cut head and neck. Rosalie's heart started to pound. There was only one Morgan from around these parts who looked like that. It was Captain, her father's horse, returning home from the war!

Rosalie squinted into the distance, looking for the figure of a man or wagon, but she saw only the horse. How could this be? Had Captain come all this way alone? Where was Father? *Where was Father*?

Rosalie squeezed her legs together and Major took off down the bumpy road. Rosalie kept her eyes fixed on Captain and, as they approached, she noticed that he seemed to have a large bundle on his back, or maybe a blanket. As they got closer, Rosalie realized with shock that the blanket covered the bony shape of a man, a tired, dirty, ragged man with his arm in a sling. Rosalie's heart was suddenly so full of love she knew it could only be one person.

"Father!" Rosalie shouted, leaping off Major. She ran to Captain and threw her arms around the horse and the man. "Father!" she said, panicking when she realized how feeble and thin he was.

Aaron Goodman lifted his head, and his feverish eyes lit up when they looked into Rosalie's. He smiled weakly. The skin of his face hung loosely, and his mustache was now more gray than black. His face looked gray, too. Rosalie was beginning to realize that her father was very sick, perhaps even close to death! Major, too, seemed to sense something was wrong. He looked at Rosalie's father curiously and touched him gently with his nose.

The Goodman fields were just on the other side of the fence lining the road. Rosalie scanned them quickly, hoping to see a sign of someone she knew.

"Help!!!" she called, cupping her hands around her mouth. "Somebody! Help!"

A small figure appeared over a rise in the field. Rosalie recognized it as her brother.

"Albert!!!" she screamed, waving her arms above her head. "Albert!" she repeated. "Come over here—NOW!"

The small figure broke into a run, quickly covering the distance between them. His face broke into a broad grin as he recognized Captain, and he joyfully hopped over the wooden fence. But he, too, stopped short when he saw what had happened to their father.

"I'm going to get Dr. Stevens," Rosalie said quickly. "Take Father home so Mother can put him to bed."

Rosalie jumped on Major and squeezed his sides with her legs. Major took off toward town, barreling down the road at high speed.

"But why can't we go in?" Mathilda asked later that evening. The three children stood in the upstairs hall outside the door to their parents' bedroom. "Is Daddy going to die?" Mathilda's face puckered up and tears rolled one after the other down her face.

Rosalie hugged her little sister tight. "Of course not!" she assured her, even though she was secretly afraid of the same thing.

"But he couldn't even walk," Albert pointed out. "When I got him home, Mama and I had to carry him up the stairs."

Rosalie gave her brother a sharp look. Albert was old enough to know not to scare their little sister. "Daddy's going to be fine," she promised.

Rosalie heard footsteps approaching the door from the other side. She clung to Mathilda, afraid of what they'd hear when the door opened.

Dr. Stevens came out first, followed by their mother. Rachel Goodman's eyes were red from crying, and her face was puffy. Did this mean they had bad news? Rosalie squeezed Mathilda tighter, bracing herself.

"Well," said Dr. Stevens,"your father's been through a very rough time. He hasn't had anything decent to eat in months and he's very weak. He also has a gunshot wound in his arm that hasn't completely healed, but it's not infected. So we won't have to amputate."

Rosalie shuddered with relief. She'd seen so many men come home from the war without an arm or a leg.

"He's going to be all right," Dr. Stevens continued. "A few months of rest and good food should bring him back to health."

Rosalie was laughing and crying at the same time. Albert was jumping up and down and Mathilda had already broken free of Rosalie and gone running into their parents' bedroom. Seeing that the doctor hadn't stopped Mathilda, Rosalie followed her sister inside.

"Just remember to be quiet around him," her mother called after her. "He can't take too much commotion."

Rosalie didn't have to be reminded. The sight of her father sitting up in bed was reminder enough of how fragile he was. He looked like little more than a skeleton with skin leaning against the fluffy white pillows, and his brown eyes looked huge in his gaunt face. But unlike before, when he'd been unable to do more than look at her, this time he smiled.

"Rosalie," he said softly, lifting his bony hand from the down coverlet. Rosalie ran to his side and gently took his hand. His skin was cool and soft.

"I love you, Daddy," she said, kissing his hand. She was longing to throw her arms around him and hug him close, but she was afraid he wasn't strong enough to withstand it. Albert and their mother gathered around the bed. Mathilda jumped up beside her father and rested her head against his shoulder.

"Mathilda," their mother warned, but Aaron shook his head. "Let her stay," he said. "The thought of this moment is the only thing that kept me alive."

"Oh, Daddy!" Rosalie said anxiously. "What happened to you? Why didn't you write?"

"I was captured in a raid at Cedar Creek," her father answered. "The Confederates took me prisoner."

Rosalie gasped, and her little sister started to cry.

"Didn't the Rebs give you anything to eat in prison?" Albert asked.

Aaron smiled wanly. "They didn't have much more than we did," he said. "It's almost all over now for the Confederates. Their supply lines are cut off and they're as weak and ragged as I am."

"Do you mean the war's almost over?" Rachel Goodman asked her husband.

Aaron nodded slowly. "I'd give it a few weeks, maybe a month."

Albert sat down on the bed beside his father. "How'd you get out?" he asked. "Did you shoot a Rebel guard and make your escape?"

Aaron laughed. "Nothing as heroic as that," he said. "They let me go. They let us all go. They couldn't feed their own men, let alone a bunch of Yankees. I had to give them most of my money to keep Captain, though. I'm happy Captain remembered the way home, 'cause I wasn't much help."

Rosalie remembered her father as she'd seen him earlier today, draped over Captain's back almost more dead than alive. He'd traveled hundreds of miles like that, with little to eat or drink and only Captain to rely on. Rosalie didn't even want to even think about how close he'd come to not making it back alive.

"But I'm here now," Aaron said, turning to look at Rosalie. "And I've heard what a good job you've been doing running the farm while I was gone."

Rosalie felt embarrassed. "I didn't run the farm," she said quickly. "Mama did."

"But *you're* the one who figured out how to save it," her mother put in. "It's a good thing I *didn't* sell the horse. The little money I would have made might have gotten us through until spring, but then we would have been without a horse. No, Rosalie's the one who saved us."

Rosalie shook her head emphatically. "It wasn't me," she insisted. "I just had an idea about renting Major, that's all. Major saved us, because he's a Morgan—and Morgans can do anything!"

EPILOGUE

A Year Passes

Miss Nelson stood with her fingertips resting on the desk in front of her. Her eyes swept the classroom as she looked for the next student to recite. Cassie, sitting to Rosalie's right, slid down a little in her seat. Erastus Woodward, sitting directly ahead of Rosalie, propped his *McGuffey's Reader* up on his desk so it hid his face.

Rosalie smiled. After all she'd been through this past year, after almost losing her home, her horse, and her father, she wasn't afraid of her teacher and she certainly wasn't afraid of reciting aloud.

Rosalie looked at her teacher until she caught her eye. Miss Nelson nodded her head in her direction.

"Rosalie Goodman," she called out. "Stand, please."

Rosalie stood straight and tall and spoke in a loud, clear voice as she recited the passage she'd memorized from *McGuffey's Reader*:

We are all here!
Father, Mother,
Sister, Brother,
All who hold each other dear.

When Rosalie was done, Miss Nelson gave a little sniff. "You may be seated," she said without praising Rosalie for her perfect recitation.

Kadiddly-dop! Kadiddly-dop! Kadiddly-dop!

Rosalie couldn't see out the window from her seat, but she didn't need to. She recognized the smart clop-clopping of Major's hooves nearing the school.

Albert, sitting near the front of the classroom, turned around and gave Rosalie a puzzled look. Rosalie, too, couldn't understand why their wagon would be heading up this road. School was almost over for the day, but it couldn't be her mother or father here to give them a ride home. She and her brother and sister always walked, rain or shine.

Rosalie began to feel anxious. Was something

wrong? Mother was expecting a baby, but not for several more months yet, at least that was what Dr. Stevens had said.

Rosalie was about to raise her hand to ask for permission to go outside when Miss Nelson rang the little bell on her desk. "Class dismissed," she said.

The room, which had been quiet but for the lone voice reciting and the occasional squeak of a wooden bench, suddenly burst to life. The aisles between the seats were filled with students racing for the cloakroom. The floorboards groaned under running booted feet. Squeals and laughter filled the air.

Rosalie threw on her cloak and grabbed her brother's and sister's hands. "Come on," she said, rushing them out the back door and down the steps.

It wasn't as Rosalie expected, her father sitting atop the wagon with a worried look on his face. Instead, Rosalie's mother held Major's reins with one hand and shielded her eyes with the other against the light of the sun. She wore Rosalie's father's rough wool overcoat because her own no longer fit her.

Rosalie ran towards the wagon, stopping to pat Major before leaping up beside her mother. "What's wrong?" she asked. "Is it the baby?"

Rachel Goodman gave Rosalie a kiss on the cheek. "My dear," she said, "you're so used to worrying, it's hard to break the habit. Nothing's wrong."

"Then why did you come for us?" Mathilda asked, clambering into the back of the wagon. Albert was already there, sticking his hand into one of several burlap sacks. Crying out with delight, he pulled out a candy stick.

Mathilda made a grab for the candy. "Let me have some!"

"There's one for each of you," Rachel called over her shoulder. "And one for Rosalie, too."

Mathilda passed the bright red candy stick to the front of the wagon. Rosalie stuck it in her mouth and sucked on it. It was cherry flavored and very sweet. "It's delicious," she told her mother. "Thank you. Now will you tell us what's going on?"

Rachel finally explained. "Your daddy and I were in town picking up supplies at Eve Decker's when who do you suppose we ran into?"

"Mrs. Green and Natalie?" Rosalie said. Natalie was the Green's new baby. She was six months old now, but so big and round most folks guessed she was much older. Natalie had a great sense of humor and laughed at everything.

"No," Rosalie's mother said, lightly flicking the reins. Major took off, not down the dirt road towards the Goodman farm, but down the other side of the hill.

Rosalie, sucking on her candy stick, began to relax. "Mr. McWalters?" she said. "If he wants to hire Major again, he'll have to pay double. Otherwise Mr. Orr gets him."

"My goodness," Rachel exclaimed, "you're quite the business expert. With all the money you're earning with Major, soon none of us will have to work."

Rosalie smiled with pride. Of course her mother was exaggerating. But Major had more offers of work than he could handle—logging, mapling, and hauling—and people were willing to pay more and more money for his services. As Major's reputation grew, so did his stud fee. That was the price people paid to have Major sire a horse with their mares.

"Not Mr. McWalters," Rachel said.

Major trotted with a brisk and light step as if he weren't pulling a heavily-loaded wagon.

"Then who?" Rosalie asked. "I give up."

Rachel Goodman's eyes gleamed mischievously. "Mr. Bober," she said.

At last Rosalie understood. Last spring, Mr. Bober had been the first to pay a stud fee for Major. And now they were heading down the hill right towards Mr. Bober's farm.

Rachel smiled. "The foal was born late last night. I

hear he's a fine, sturdy little fellow."

Rosalie began hopping up and down on the wagon's hard wooden seat. She couldn't wait a second longer to see Major's first offspring. "Giddyap, Major!" she shouted.

Moments later Rosalie, her mother, brother, sister and Major arrived at their neighbor's barn. Rosalie's father, Aaron, was already there with Mr. Bober.

"Daddy!" Rosalie cried, running to him. "Where is he? Where is he?" Aaron Goodman's hair was gray now, as was the bushy beard he'd grown since his return from the war. The spot on his arm where the bullet passed through still ached on rainy days. But in all other respects he was the same man Rosalie remembered from before the war. Tall, strong, and broad-shouldered with a ready smile and a deep, booming laugh.

He laughed now. "He's inside with his mother. Patience, Rosalie, patience."

Mr. Bober went into the barn and returned with Juniper, a mixed-breed mare. By her side was her foal, still wobbly on its long, spindly legs. Major's son was a bay, just like him, with a broad neck and shoulders which hinted at the power to come.

The foal nuzzled against his mother as Major took a few steps forward and lowered his head to sniff and get a closer look at his son. Seemingly pleased, he raised his head and gave a loud whinny.

Rosalie gave Major a big hug. "Congratulations!" she said, kissing his neck. "You're a daddy!"

Rosalie beamed with happiness for Major, for herself, for everybody. After all the wonderful things Major had done, he had the reward he deserved. A family!

FACTS
ABOUT THE BREED

You probably know a lot about Morgans from reading this book. Here are some more interesting facts about this hearty American breed.

∩ Morgans generally stand between 14.2 and 15.2 hands high. Instead of using feet and inches, all horses are measured in hands. A hand is equal to four inches.

∩ Morgans are usually bay (brown with a black mane, tail, and lower leg), chestnut (reddish brown all over), brown, or black. Sometimes Morgans are buckskin (golden-tan with black mane, tail, and lower leg), palomino (gold with a white mane and tail), or gray.

∩ A horse cannot be registered with the

Morgan Horse Association if it has any white on its legs or body above the knees. White on the face is acceptable, but the horse must not have blue eyes.

∩ Morgans have small, alert ears and thick, silky manes and tails. Their eyes are generally large and wide set. Like the Arabian, the Morgan often carries its tail high.

∩ Morgans are well known for their strong and well-developed muscles. Their backs tend to be short, and their hind quarters are well rounded.

∩ The Morgan is America's oldest breed. Morgan horses have helped to develop several other breeds of horse, including the Tennessee Walking Horse, and the Standardbred.

∩ Morgans get their name from their foundation sire, or founding father, Justin Morgan. The Morgan is the only breed that is named after one individual horse.

∩ Justin Morgan was born in 1789. As a colt, he was called Figure, and his owner was named Justin Morgan. Eventually, the small bay horse, who stood only 14.2 hands, became known by the man's name.

∩ A statue at the Morgan Horse Farm at the University of Vermont in Shelburne, Vt., commemorates the life and great achievements of the horse Justin Morgan. He was famous for his ability to out-pull, out-run, and out-work any other horse. There is even a book about him!

∩ Justin Morgan was also a well-mannered horse. He once calmly carried President James Monroe through a busy military parade ground.

∩ Many of Justin Morgan's decendents are famous, too. His great-grandson Ethan Allen was the fastest trotting horse in New England at the end of the 1800s.

∩ Morgans were used by the U.S. Army as cavalry horses before the development of machinery. They are still favored as police mounts because they are strong and even tempered.

∩ Today most Morgans are bred for their showy qualities. They are used as fine harness horses, as saddle seat mounts, and as high-stepping park horse competitors.

∩ Morgans are still very versatile horses. Many Morgans compete in three day events, in the dressage ring, and as hunters.

∩ Some Morgans barrel race, others compete in trotting races, and still others make kind and gentle family horses. Morgans really can do it all!